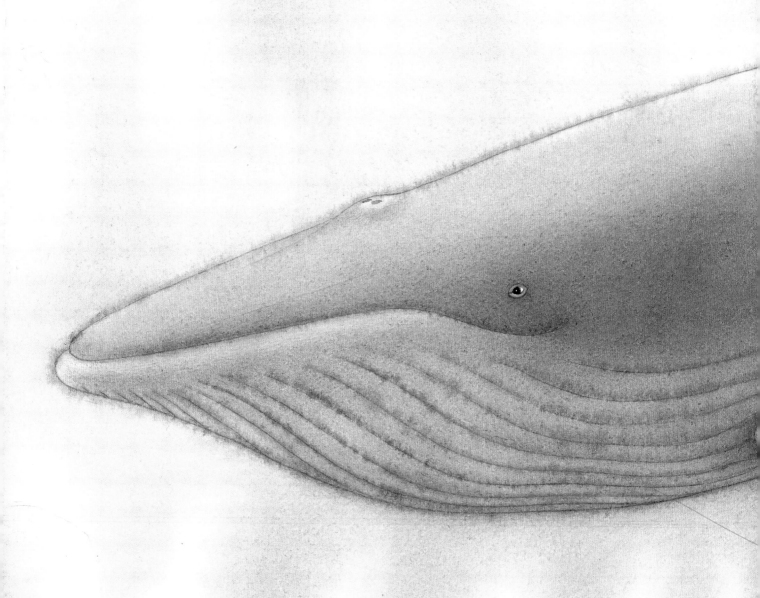

FOR DAVY SIDJANSKI

Coventry City Council	
CEN*	
3 8002 02326 263 9	
Askews & Holts	Feb-2017
	£6.99

First published in the United States, Great Britain, Canada,
Australia, and New Zealand in 1998 by North-South Books Inc., New York 10016,
an imprint of NordSüd Verlag AG, CH-8005 Zürich, Switzerland.
Distributed in the United States by North-South Books Inc., New York 10016.
First paperback edition published in Great Britain, Australia and New Zealand in 2008.

Library of Congress Cataloging-in-Publication Data is available.

A CIP catalogue record for this book is available from The British Library.

ISBN: 978-0-7358-1009-9 (trade edition)
7 9 11 13 HC 14 12 10 8
ISBN: 978-3-314-01669-1 (paperback edition)
7 9 11 PB 10 8 6
Printed in China by ColorPrint Offset, November 2014

www.northsouth.com

Meet Marcus Pfister at www.marcuspfister.ch

FSC
www.fsc.org
MIX
Paper from
responsible sources
FSC® C007972

MARCUS PFISTER is the author of the phenomenally successful Rainbow Fish series, as well as many other books for children. He has worked as a graphic artist, a sculptor, a painter, and a photographer as well as a children's book creator.

North
South

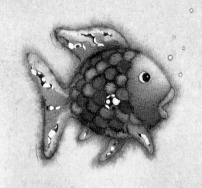

MARCUS PFISTER

RAINBOW FISH
AND THE BIG BLUE WHALE

TRANSLATED BY J. ALISON JAMES

North
South

A long way out in the deep blue sea,
Rainbow Fish and his friends swam happily
through the reef. Each of them had a glittering
silver scale—except for one little striped fish,
but he belonged to the group anyway.

When the fish were hungry, they ate tiny krill. There seemed to be endless supplies of the delicious shrimp. Rainbow Fish only needed to glide gently through the water with his mouth open to catch as many as he wanted. It was a wonderful life.

One day a gentle old whale swam by the reef and decided to stay. He liked the spot, since he too ate the krill that were so plentiful there. And he enjoyed being around the glittering fish. Often he drifted along, watching them for hours, admiring their beautiful silvery scales.

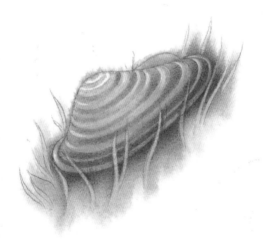

Before long, the fish with the jagged fins
noticed the whale watching them.
   "Why is he looking at us like that?" he asked
the others. He was in a particularly bad mood
that day. "See how he's staring at us?" he went
on irritably. "Who knows what he's thinking?"

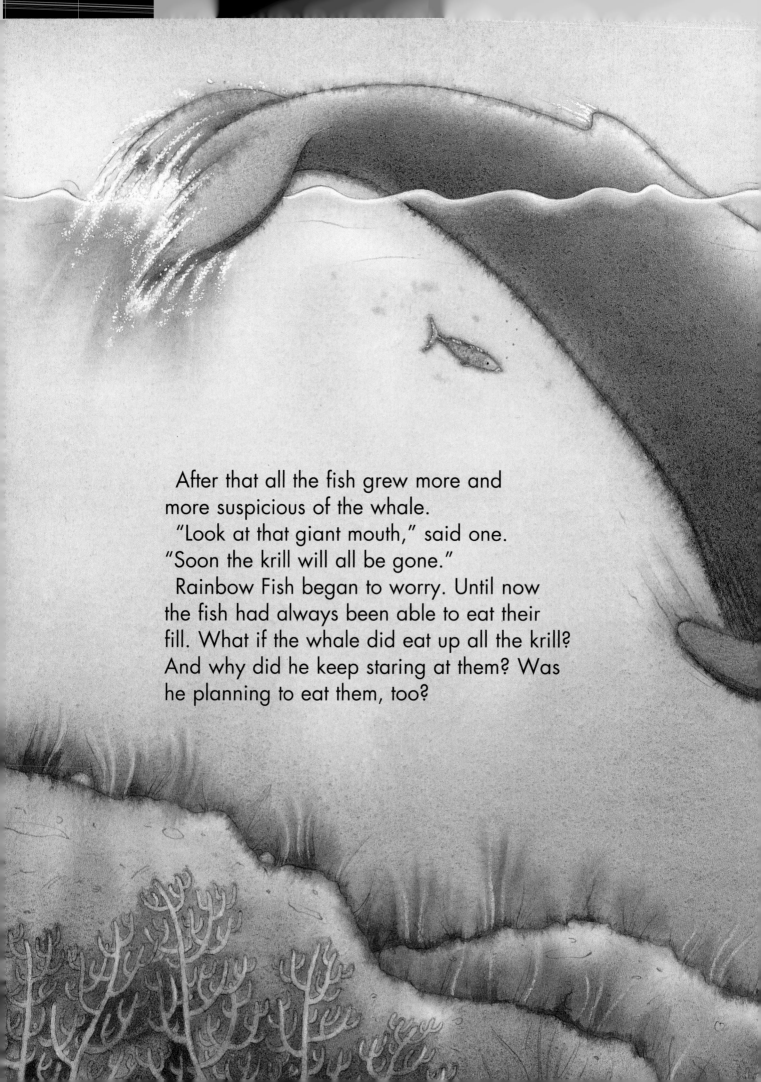

After that all the fish grew more and
more suspicious of the whale.
  "Look at that giant mouth," said one.
"Soon the krill will all be gone."
  Rainbow Fish began to worry. Until now
the fish had always been able to eat their
fill. What if the whale did eat up all the krill?
And why did he keep staring at them? Was
he planning to eat them, too?

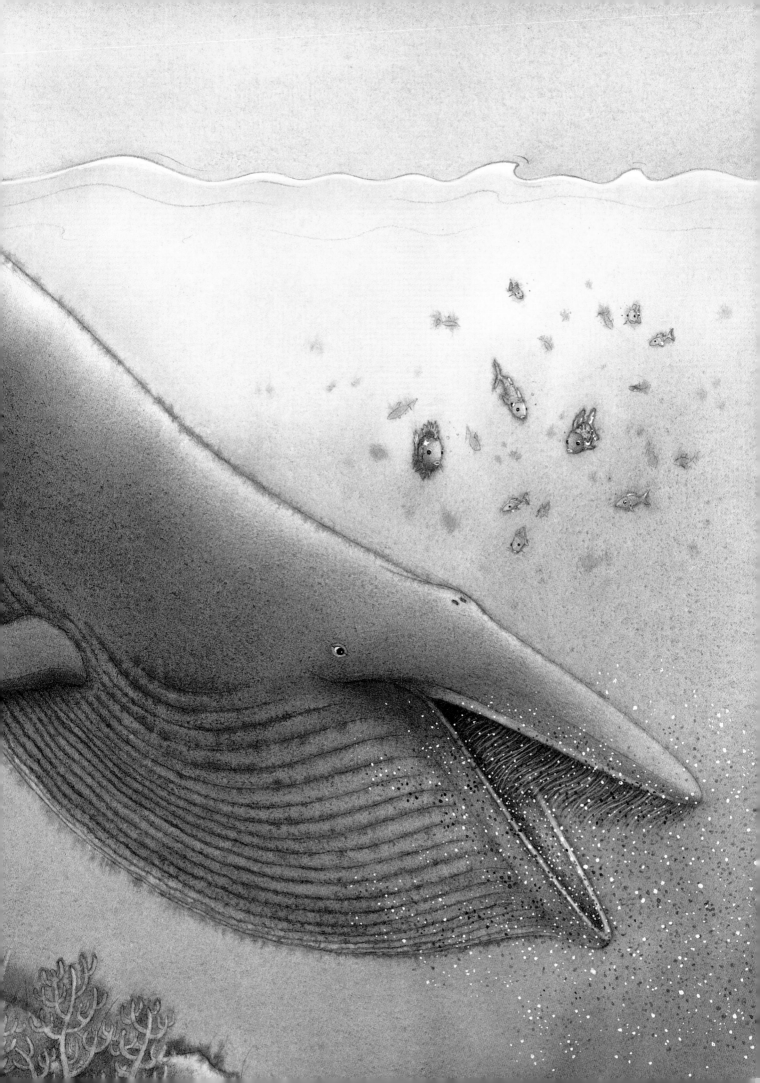

One day the whale swam quite near the
school of glittering fish. Panicked, the fish with
the jagged fins sounded the alarm.

"Look out!" he called. "The wicked whale is
after us!"

When the whale heard that, he was hurt at
first, but soon he grew very angry.

I'll show them! he thought. I'll teach them a
lesson!

So the great blue whale shot into the middle
of the school and lashed out with his gigantic
tail, sweeping the sparkling fish in all directions.

The terrified fish fled, racing towards a crack in the reef for safety. But the whale didn't leave them alone. He followed Rainbow Fish and his friends all the way back to their cave.

The blue whale swam back and forth,
casting sinister glances at the little fish.
   They were trapped!
   "I told you that whale was dangerous,"
whispered the fish with the jagged fins.
"We have to watch out for him!"
   After a while the whale calmed down.
He made one last pass, then disappeared
behind the reef.

Nervous, but driven by hunger, the fish
cautiously left their cave and swam off in search
of food. But the battle with the whale had left its
mark: all the krill had been driven off.

"This is silly!" declared Rainbow Fish. "Before,
we played happily in the sea. Now we hide
in terror in our cave. Before, there was always
enough food for everyone. Now we have
nothing. We must make peace with the whale."

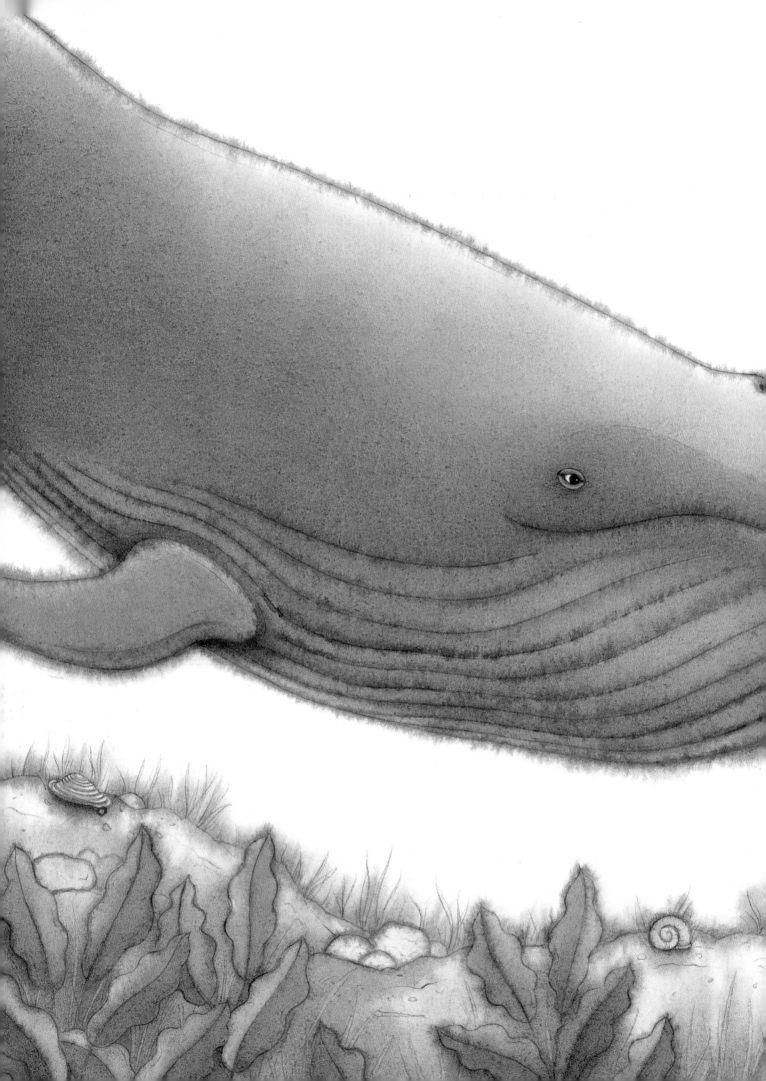

The other fish were all too afraid to approach the whale. It was up to Rainbow Fish.

The whale stared at Rainbow Fish suspiciously.

"Please, let's talk," said Rainbow Fish. "This fight was all a big mistake. It drove off the krill and now we're all hungry."

The two talked for a long time.

The whale told Rainbow Fish how hurt and angry their hostile words had made him. "I never meant to harm you," said the whale, "just scare you a little."

Rainbow Fish was ashamed. "I'm sorry," he said. "But when we saw you watching us all the time, we were afraid you might eat us."

The whale looked surprised. "I watched you only because your shining scales are so pretty," he said.

They both laughed.

"Come now," said the whale. "Let's find new hunting grounds."

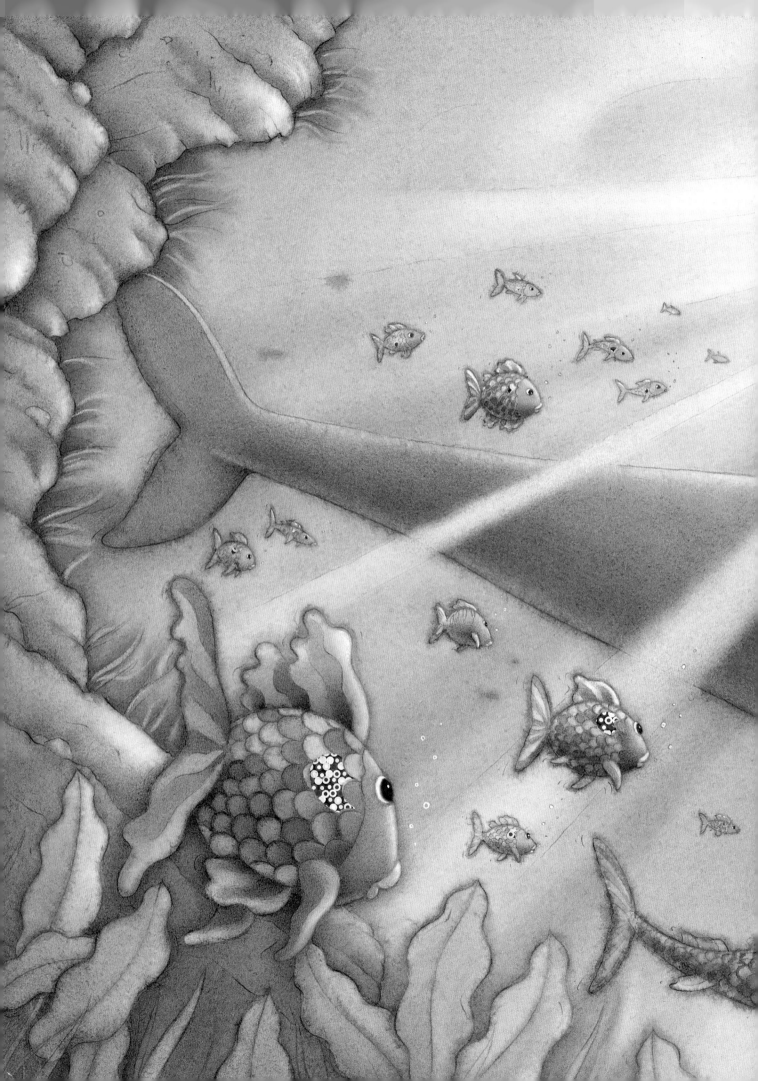

So Rainbow Fish and his friends, protected by their new friend the big blue whale, swam off together in search of a new home rich with krill. And before long, none of them could remember what the terrible fight had been about.

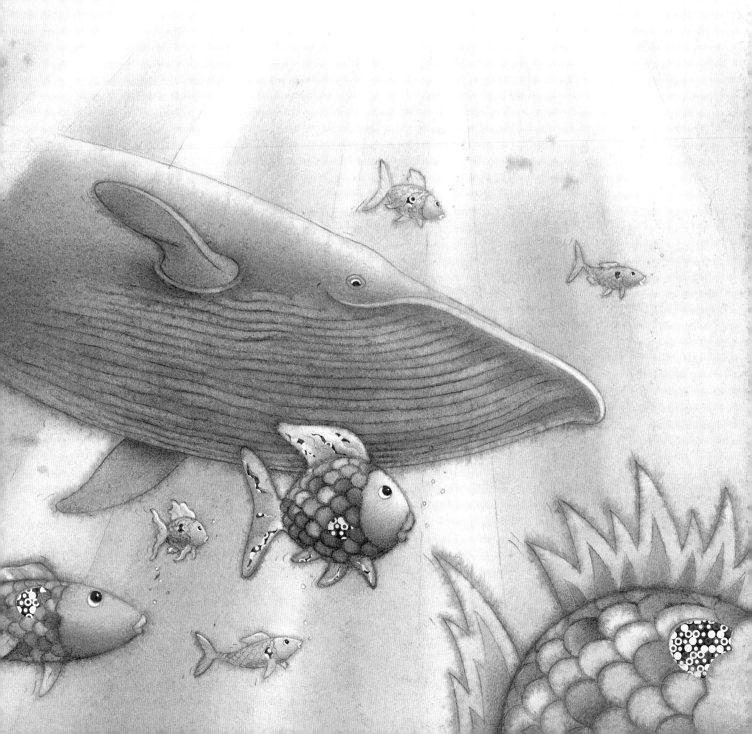

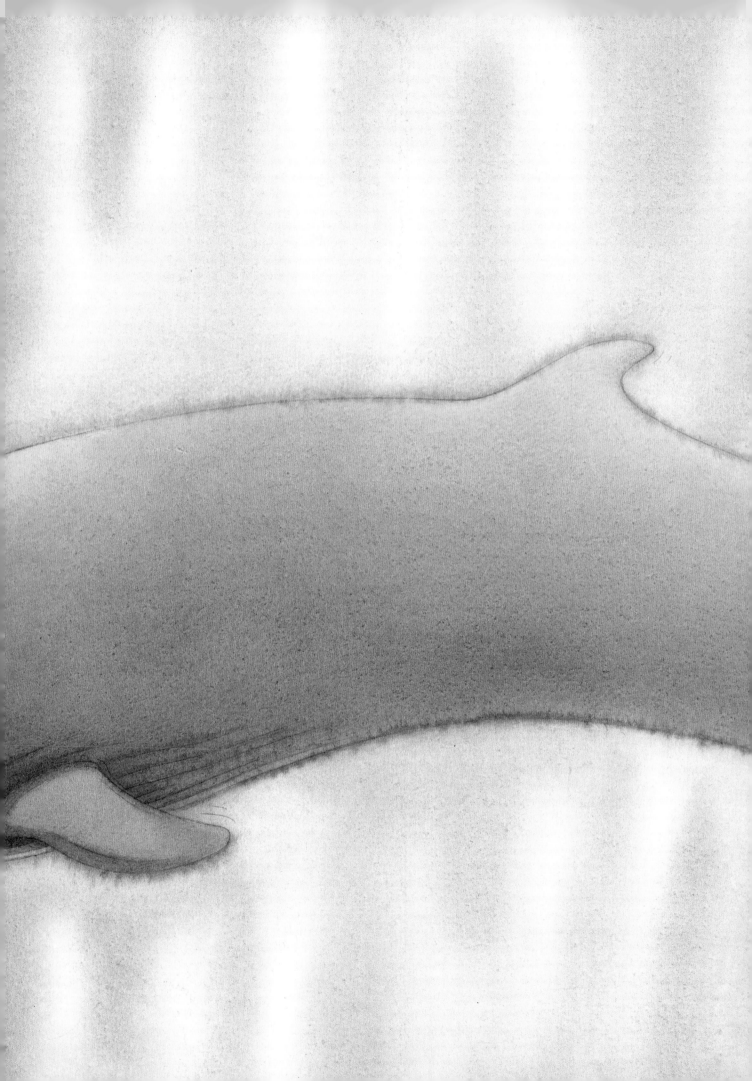

Read all the Rainbow Fish Adventures: